In Level 0, **Step 4** builds on the previous steps and introduces their letters:

e   u   r   h   b

Special features:

Phonically decodable text builds reading confidence

Short sentences with simple language

Repetition of sounds in different words

Ross, Gus and Miss Hill get off the bus.

Miss Hill tells Gus it is hot in the sun.

Put a hat on!

No!

22

23

Story Words
Can you match these words to the pictures?

Gus
Ross
bus
Miss Hill
hat
sun
log
net

30

Tricky Words

These tricky words are in the story you have just read. They cannot be phonetically sounded out.
Can you memorize them and read them super fast?

the
to
into
I

31

Summary page to reinforce learning

Practice of words that cannot be sounded out

Phonics and Book Banding Consultant: Kate Ruttle

LADYBIRD BOOKS

UK | USA | Canada | Ireland | Australia
India | New Zealand | South Africa

Ladybird Books is part of the Penguin Random House group of companies
whose addresses can be found at global.penguinrandomhouse.com.

www.penguin.co.uk www.puffin.co.uk www.ladybird.co.uk

A version of this book was previously published as
Huff! Puff! Run! – Ladybird I'm Ready for Phonics: Level 4, 2014
This edition published 2018
003

Printed in China

A CIP catalogue record for this book is available from the British Library

ISBN: 978–0–241–31251–3

All correspondence to
Ladybird Books
Penguin Random House Children's
80 Strand, London WC2R 0RL

The Fun Run

Written by Monica Hughes
Illustrated by Chris Jevons

Gus, Ross, Mum and Dad go to the fun run.

Gus has a lot of kit.

I am fit!

Ross has no kit and is
fed up.

Miss Hill sets off the fun run. Mum and Dad tell Gus to run and run.

Ross is at the back.

I am sad.
I am at
the back.

Gus runs off but gets hot and has a nap.

Ross gets hot but runs on.

Ross gets back to Miss Hill.
Ross gets a medal.

Gus gets up.

Gus gets back and gets
his medal.

15

Story Words

Can you match these words
to the pictures?

Gus   Miss Hill

Ross   nap

fun run   medal

Tricky Words

These tricky words are in the story you have just read. They cannot be sounded out. Can you memorize them and read them super fast?

to

the

go

I

no

Gus is Hot!

Written by Monica Hughes
Illustrated by Chris Jevons

Miss Hill, Gus and Ross get on the bus.

Gus runs to the back
of the bus.

Ross, Gus and Miss Hill
get off the bus.

Miss Hill tells Gus it is
hot in the sun.

Ross and Gus sit on logs.
Ross dips his net into
the bog.

Gus rams his net into the bog.

25

Ross has a net. It is
full of big bugs.

Gus tugs up his net
and it is full of mud.

Back on the bus, Gus is ill.

Story Words

Can you match these words to the pictures?

Gus

Ross

bus

Miss Hill

hat

sun

log

net